Sniffer at the Coronation

Pippa Pennington

Illustrated by Eitatsu

and Merl Rehman

Cover by Nifty Illustration

Reading and story time is all about having fun. A crown is hidden in every picture. See how many you can find.

Mr and Mrs Love were putting things in the car. "We must be going somewhere," Sniffer said. "I'm going to get in the car now."

"You'd better wait and see," his mum said.

Sniffer didn't listen. He climbed into the car and fell asleep.

Mr Love shut the car door. Mrs Love called out to Sniffer and his mum. "Be good. We'll be back later."

Mr Love started the car.

Mr and Mrs Love didn't see Sniffer asleep in the back of the car. Oh no!

Sniffer was asleep all the way to London. Mr Love stopped the car. Mr and Mrs Love went to the back of the car. Sniffer jumped out of the door.

Sniffer's nose went up in the air. Sniff. Sniff. Sniff. Phew! What is that?

Sniffer trotted along the path. London was very busy and he knew he had to stay on the path. A big, red bus went past. Sniffer didn't want to go near the bus.

Phew! That bus is smelly.

Sniffer's nose went up in the air. Phew! What is that? He had to find out what was making such a smelly smell. A man was cooking burgers with onions. Sniffer liked the smell of the burger. The onions smelled bad.

Sniffer was hungry.

Sniffer looked at a little boy who had a burger. Sniff. Sniff. Sniff. The burger smelled good. Sniffer went closer.

Oh no! Don't do it, Sniffer!

The smell was so good. Sniffer grabbed the burger and he ran. The little boy shouted. The man shouted. They chased Sniffer.

Sniffer ran and ran.

Sniffer hid behind a big wall and ate the burger. "Hey! Are you going to share that?" Sniffer looked up and saw a dog. Sniffer was frightened. He dropped the burger.

"Cor, thank you," the dog said. "Jolly decent of you."

The dog ate the burger. "You have to watch out for the dog catcher," the dog said. Sniffer had some trouble with the dog catcher at the beach.

"Is he near here?" Sniffer asked.

"Tell you what. You stick with me and we'll be fine." The dog put his nose in the air. "I'm connected to the royal family. I can pretty much do as I like around here."

"Phew! What is that smell?" Sniffer asked.

"Come on," said the dog. "I'll show you." They trotted around a corner and saw lots of fish for sale.

"Smelly fish," the dog said. "Do you want one?"

The dog took a fish and ran. Sniffer ran after him. A lady shouted and ran after them.

Sniffer and the dog stopped to share the fish. "Phew! What is that?" Sniffer asked.

"The horses. They always smell like that," the dog said. Sniffer and the dog watched the horses walk past.

"Why are the men dressed like that?" Sniffer asked.

"The royal coronation, of course," the dog said.

The horses had nearly gone. "What's the royal coronation?" Sniffer asked.

The dog shook his head. "My owner is the king. Today he gets his crown," he said. "Come on. I'll take you to the palace."

Sniffer and the dog trotted after the horses.

There were so many people, Sniffer stayed close to the dog. People waved flags. "Phew! I can smell horses again," Sniffer said.

Four horses pulled a carriage. The people cheered. "Hooray! Hooray!"

"Quick in the gates. Follow me," the dog said.

Sniffer followed the dog into the palace. Sniff. Sniff. Sniff. "Cor! What is that?" Sniffer said.

"We have the best kitchen in the country," the dog said. "This way."

Sniffer was excited. He'd never smelled anything so good.

The dog went through a door. Sniffer stopped and looked at something strange. It smelled good.

Oh no! That's the coronation cake. Don't do it, Sniffer!

Sniffer went closer. Sniff. Sniff. Sniff. "That looks just like a bone," he said. "I bet it tastes good."

He opened his mouth and pulled the bone.

Splat! The cake fell on Sniffer.

"Oh no! What happened?" Sniffer said.

A man ran through the door. "Hey! Oh no!" he shouted. "The cake!"

The man looked very cross.

The King waved. Everyone cheered. "Hooray! Hooray!

Oh no! Who can you see with cake on his head and a cherry on his nose?

Sniffer ran. The chef chased him. Mr and Mrs Love looked. "Oh dear! That dog looks like Sniffer," Mrs Love said.

"It's not Sniffer," Mr Love said. "Sniffer is at home."

Sniffer ran back past the horses,
back past the fish market,
back past the burger stall,
and back past the bus.

Sniffer ran all the way back to the car. He sat down to wait for Mr and Mrs Love. He hoped they came back soon.

London was a scary place. He only wanted to do a bit of sniffing.

Mr and Mrs Love saw the car. "What is that next to the car?" Mr Love said.

"It's Sniffer," Mrs Love said. "Oh, Sniffer! How did you get here?"

Sniffer opened his eyes. He wagged his tail. He was happy to see Mr and Mrs Love.

"What is that on his nose?" Mrs Love said.

"It's a cherry," Mr Love said. "And that is cake icing all over his head!"

Mrs Love looked cross. "Oh, Sniffer! What have you done?"

Mrs Love rubbed the cake off of Sniffer.

Mrs Love shouted.

Mr Love shouted.

Sniffer curled up on the back seat of the car. They didn't need to shout. He only wanted that lovely, smelly, white bone.

Sniffer closed his eyes and went to sleep. He dreamed of London. The bus, the burger, the lions, the chef and his friend, the dog.

When he woke up they were at home. Sniffer was happy. He never wanted to go sniffing again.

The next morning the sun was shining. Sniffer opened his eyes. Sniff. Sniff. Sniff. Phew! What is that?

Oh no! What do you think Sniffer will do next?

Other books by Pippa Pennington

Picture Books

Sniffer: the little dog who loves to sniff

Sniffer at the Beach

Sniffer at the Farm

Sniffer's First Christmas

Sniffer goes on Holiday

Sniffer at the Zoo

Sniffer's First Halloween

Sniffer Rhyming Books (these run alongside the picture books)

Phew! What's that smell? (Book 1)

Phew! What's that smell at the Beach? (Book 2)

Phew! What's that smell at the Farm? (Book 3)

Phew! What's that smell at Christmas? (Book 4)

Phew! What's that smell on Holiday? (Book 5)

Starting to read with Sniffer

Book 1 This is Sniffer...

Book 2 Sniffer likes...

Book 3 Sniffer can see...

Book 4 Sniffer can smell...

Book 5 Where is Sniffer?

Printed in Great Britain
by Amazon

21916787R00018